CAPTAIN CRUNCHY
SECRET CODE

1	2	3	4	5	6
A	B	C	D	E	F

7	8	9	10	11	12
G	H	I	J	K	L

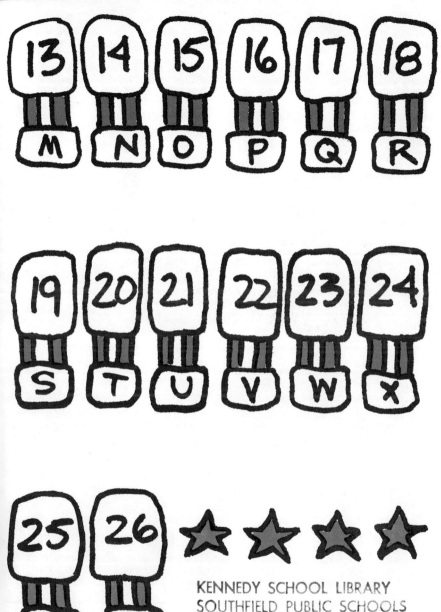

AMY
FOR
SHORT

by Laura Joffe Numeroff

MACMILLAN PUBLISHING CO., INC.

New York

COLLIER MACMILLAN PUBLISHERS

London

FOR MY PARENTS, WITH LOVE
With special thanks to
Elizabeth Shub,
Alan Benjamin,
Barbara Bottner and
Bart Pepitone

Macmillan Publishing Co., Inc.
866 Third Avenue, New York, N.Y. 10022
Collier Macmillan Canada, Ltd.
Printed in the United States of America
10   9   8   7   6   5   4   3   2   1

LIBRARY OF CONGRESS CATALOGING IN PUBLICATION DATA

Numeroff, Laura Joffe.
  Amy for short.

  (Ready-to-read)
  SUMMARY: When she grows taller than Mark, Amy
is afraid he doesn't want to be best friends anymore.
  [1. Friendship—Fiction] I. Title.
PZ7.N964Am3   [E]   76–8842
ISBN 0–02–768180–7

Contents

"Treetops"
5

Camp
18

The Birthday
28

"TREETOPS"

My name is Amelia Ann Valerie
Sue Virginia Lee Brandon.

Amy for short.

But I'm tall.

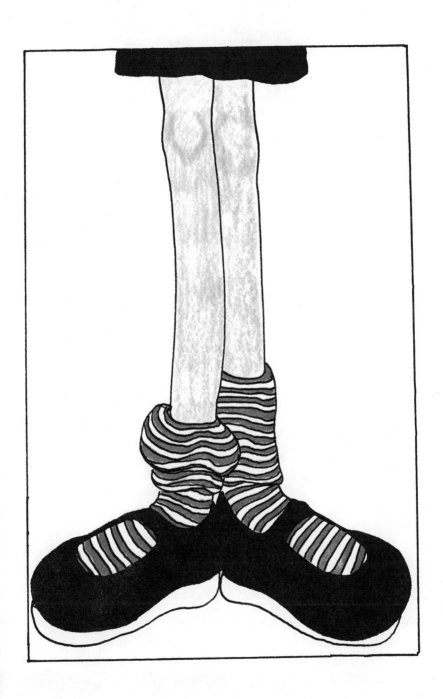

Very.

I'm the tallest girl in my class,
so I always have to stand
at the back of the line.
Sometimes the kids call me
"Stringbean" or "Beanpole."

Usually they call me "Treetops."
So for Halloween, I was a tree.

Mark is as tall as I am, but
no one calls him "Stringbean"
or "Beanpole."
He's the blackboard monitor
and my best friend.
He lives on the same
block as I do.
He has a lizard named Fred
and a cat named Harriet.
(Harriet hates Fred.)

On Halloween, Mark was
the Empire State Building.

We spend time together
without talking.

We had matching sweaters
and matching caps.
But I lost my cap.
We're both saving up for
a Captain Crunchy
Secret Decoder Ring.
So far we have 58¢.

For Christmas, Mark gave me
a box of clay.
I made a clay ashtray, a clay bird,
and a clay bowl for Mark's birthday.
I was going to make a clay dish
for my mother, but...

I gave up clay and
took up painting.

CAMP

The summer after second grade,

Mark went to the country.

I went to Camp Ta-Koo-Mi-Noo-Chee.

I was the tallest girl in my bunk.

I signed up for arts and

crafts and hiking and nature.

We played "Capture the Flag"

and kickball.

I captured the flag but

forgot to bring it back.

19

The third week of camp,

we put on a play.

I was Abe Lincoln.

Mark and I were still friends
by mail. Though sometimes
I couldn't read his handwriting.
It sure would have been handy
to have a Captain Crunchy
Secret Decoder Ring.
But we still had 92¢ more
to save up.

July 14

Amy,

My grandmother's house

has a million rooms.

Some are good for hiding.

But there is no one to hide from.

The lake has fish in it.

I caught ten grasshoppers,

three flies, two salamanders,

and a cricket.

His name is Bart.

My cousin Harold is no fun.

He doesn't even know what a

Captain Crunchy

Secret Decoder Ring is!

Mark

July 18

Mark,

I can't wait to see the cricket.
We're learning all about snakes
in nature class.
My counselor fainted.
Last night we had chocolate
pudding for dessert.
I traded my hamburger for Emily's
chocolate pudding.
The counselor made us trade back.
Alice fell out of bed last week.

Amy

23

Two things were different
when I got home.
My turtle Howie was
bigger. And I was an
inch taller than Mark.

Every five minutes he'd say,
"Let's measure again."
We must have measured
a million times.
We measured back to back.
We measured with a ruler,
a piece of string,
a tape measure, and my
"Watch Me Grow" chart.

Now it was easier for me
to reach important things
like the cookie jar.
And the cereal boxes.
(They are usually on the top shelf.)
When I went shopping with
my mother, I could see
what prizes were in
the cereal boxes.

Mark was standing on his
tiptoes a lot.
He even started calling me
"Treetops."
I was afraid he wasn't
going to be my best friend
any more, just because I
was taller than he was.

THE BIRTHDAY

My eighth birthday was coming up
in two weeks.
My mother said I could have a
party with lots of cake and
ice cream and balloons.
She took the "Pin the Tail
on the Donkey" game out of the closet.
I practiced, but mostly I
ended up at his nose.

I invited ten of my friends:
Roz, Hilarie, Cheryl, Ricky, Steven,
Cynthia, Alyse, Douglas, Nancy,
and Mark.
Cynthia lives next door to me.
I had to invite her.
I even had special invitations
with clowns on them
to send in the mail.
I addressed the envelopes.

My mother said we should
write "R.S.V.P." on the invitations.
I thought it meant "Really
Special Valentine Party."
She said it meant
something in French.
You're supposed to call or write and
tell the person that you're coming.
Or that you're not.
I said none of my friends
would know what it meant.
She said their mothers would.

Everyone called except Mark.

I was sure he didn't want to be

my best friend any more.

Everyone was coming except Steven.

He had the measles.

I said I'd mail him some cake.

(Even Cynthia was coming!)

I asked my mother if I
could forget about the
R.S.V.P. and just call Mark.
She said O.K.

When I called him, he told me
he thought R.S.V.P. meant
"Really Scary Vampire Party."
He said he couldn't come
because he had to pitch
for a Little League game.
He said it was very important
for him to strike out Waynie Phillips.
(Waynie Phillips is the biggest kid
in the whole third grade.)

I tried to figure out
a way to cancel the party.
What's a birthday party
without your best friend?
I asked my mother if we could
forget about the party.
"Amy, what would you tell
your friends who are coming?"
"I could say I wasn't having
a birthday this year."
"I think it's too late to
change it, dear.
Don't worry about Mark."
I did anyway. A lot.

The day of my party,
I woke up feeling sad.
I didn't know why.
Then I remembered that
Mark wasn't coming.
Usually I'm up extra
early on my birthday.
Sometimes so early that not
even the Early, Early Bird
Cartoons are on yet.

I tried to go back to sleep.
Maybe I could sleep through
the whole party.

If I pretended my stomach hurt,
maybe we wouldn't
have to have the party.
But then there wouldn't be
any cake, either.
I knew it was going to be
a terrible party.
Terrible, terrible, terrible.

While we were eating breakfast,

the doorbell rang.

I was so busy worrying about Mark,

I didn't even hear it.

My mother asked me to

see who was at the door.

It was probably the lady

delivering the cake.

We had ordered a pink cake

with red flowers on it,

and my name, too.

I opened the door,

but nobody was there.

I looked all around.

On the top step was a box

with a note attached.

The note said,

9-6/9-20/9-19-14-20/
2-15-15/12-1-20-5/1-13/
9/19-20-9-12-12/
9-14-22-9-20-5-4?
9/13-1-14/2-5-1-20/
23-1-25-14-9-5/
16-8-9-12-12-9-16-19/
1-14-25/15-12-4/20-9-13-5/,
13-1-18-6

I ripped off the wrapping
paper and opened the box.
In the box was another box.
In that box was a plastic egg.

I opened the plastic egg.

In the egg there was a lump

of tissue paper tied up in string.

I untied the string.

I took out something wrapped in

more tissue paper.

I figured it was a trick.

I couldn't decide whether

to continue opening it up.

I didn't want to spend all

morning opening boxes.

I continued anyway.

I unwrapped the tissue paper—

and there was a Captain Crunchy

Secret Decoder Ring!

I ran inside to tell my mother.

Then I asked her to help

me break the code.

I couldn't wait to read the message.

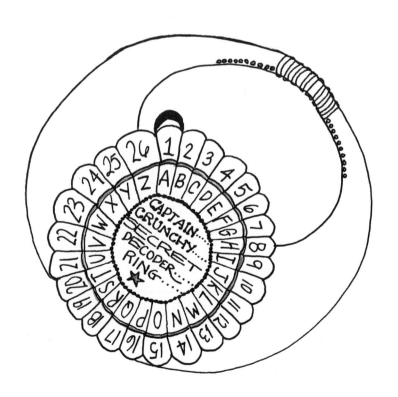

I got a piece of paper

and a pencil for my mother.

I held the ring.

My mother read the numbers out loud.

After a few minutes,

we had the message.

It said, "If it isn't too late,
am I still invited?
I can beat Waynie Phillips
any old time. Mark."